DISASTER DIARIES

ROBOTS!

DISASTER DIARIES

Zombies!

Aliens!

Brainwashed!

Robots!

ROBOTS!

R. McGEDDON

[Imprint]
MAKE YOUR MARK

NEW YORK

Special thanks to Barry Hutchison

[Imprint]
MAKE YOUR MARK

A part of Macmillan Children's Publishing Group, LLC

Library of Congress Cataloging-in-Publication Data is available.
ISBN 978-1-250-13562-9 (hardcover) / ISBN 978-1-250-13563-6 (ebook)

Our books may be purchased in bulk for promotional, educational, or
business use. Please contact your local bookseller or the Macmillan
Corporate and Premium Sales Department at (800) 221-7945 ext. 5442
or by e-mail at MacmillanSpecialMarkets@macmillan.com.

Imprint logo designed by Amanda Spielman

First edition—2017

10 9 8 7 6 5 4 3 2

mackids.com

Do you know what robots do to swindlers
Who snatch up books they know aren't theirs?
They laser-blast those thieves to cinders
Till all that's left are bones and hairs!

FOR THE DALEKS, THE INSPIRATION TO
RAMPAGING ROBOTS EVERYWHERE

CHAPTER ONE

It was the day of the school science fair, and the eyes of the world had once more turned on the sleepy town of Sitting Duck.

Well, not the whole world, obviously. That would be silly. Everyone in the *whole world* hadn't gathered together to watch a small school science fair. They wouldn't all fit in the hall for a start, and the line for the bathrooms would have been a mile long.

In fact, if I'm honest, there were mostly just teachers and students wandering around making the place look untidy—but if you hold your school science fair in a school, what else can you expect?

Tables were lined up inside the hall, each one

displaying a different project. A lot of them were modeling-clay volcanoes that fizzed white foam out of the top when you poured vinegar in. But, in an interesting twist, one was white foam that supposedly shot vinegar out of the top when you dropped a volcano in. Although no one had thought to bring a volcano with them, so it couldn't be put to the test.

As well as all that stuff, there was one thing even more important in the school hall that day— friendship. And heroes.

Okay, that's two things.

In fact, here come a couple of those friendly heroes now: Sam Saunders and Emmie Lane.

What can I say about Sam that hasn't already been said? Well, he's probably about your height, actually, or maybe a bit smaller. Or taller.

Depends what height you are, really. He's roughly around your height—let's just say that.

Sam loves sports. Like, really loves them. Whether it's baseball, football, soccer, basketball, or dodgeball, he can't get enough of that stuff. When he's not playing sports, he's hanging out with his best friends, being liked by everyone he meets, and *saving the frickin' world*!

Emmie, I'll be honest, isn't liked by everyone. But that's fine, because she doesn't really like everyone, either. It works out quite well, actually, as it means most people try to avoid talking to her in case she shouts at them or something.

Her hobbies include being angry, plotting elaborate escapes from her great-aunt Doris's house, and leaving sarcastic comments on YouTube videos. Oh, and *saving the frickin' world*!

Sam and Emmie were strutting like a pair of champions through the hall, clutching their own science projects and checking out the competition. As they approached one table, a creature with a dozen eyes popped up from behind it and let out a high-pitched squeal. Instinctively, Emmie lunged at it, ready to wrestle the thing to the ground, but Sam caught her just in time.

"Relax," he said. "It's just Phoebe."

"Like, of course," said Phoebe. "And what do you mean 'just' Phoebe?"

Phoebe Bowles was Emmie's all-time worst enemy, and considering Emmie had recently battled a power-hungry mad scientist with a brainwashing machine, that was really saying something. Emmie was very much your average running-around, climbing-trees, punching-supervillains-in-the-face type of person, while Phoebe loved nothing more than . . . well, herself, really.

"What are you wearing?" Emmie asked, her eyes drawn to Phoebe's hat. It was a fluffy blue

beret, but sticking out from it at all angles were six metal arms. At the end of each arm dangled a little mirror, making it look like a hundred eyes were reflecting outward.

"It's a rotating mirror hat," sniffed Phoebe, like it was the most obvious thing in the world.

"What's a rotating mirror hat?" asked Sam.

"Are you kidding me?" Phoebe snorted. "It's, like, a hat with mirrors on it. So you can see yourself from every angle. It's my science project."

Sam spotted Emmie's fists clenching.

"Right!" he said. "Good luck with that."

"What have you made?" Phoebe asked. "Something lame, I bet."

Sam produced a deodorant can and sprayed it into the air. Phoebe sniffed, then immediately stumbled back, clutching her nose and mouth.

"Eww! It smells like
something died!" she said,
grimacing.

"Exactly," said Sam.
"It's antizombie deodorant.
One spray and you can pass
yourself off as one of the living dead!"

"Why would you want to do that?" asked Phoebe.

"In case zombies ever come back," said Sam.

Phoebe frowned. "Zombies?"

"Yeah," said Sam. "Like last time? Remember?"

Phoebe stared blankly at him.

"Hundreds of them. Arms dropping off and
stuff," Sam continued.

Phoebe shook her head.

"You turned into one," said Emmie. "And ate
an old woman."

"Oh, *that* time," said Phoebe. "Gotcha." She turned to Emmie, peering down her nose. "What did you make?"

Emmie held up what looked like a TV remote. "It's an alien detector."

"Aliens?" said Phoebe. "There's no such thing."

Emmie and Sam exchanged a glance.

"Yeah, well, if they ever do turn up, an alarm in this thing will go off," Emmie said.

Suddenly, the alien detector came to life, and a very loud alarm rang out. So loud, in fact, that half a dozen volcanoes erupted throughout the hall.

"Shut that

thing up!" yelped Mr. Nerdgoober, a science teacher who definitely had a bit of an alien look about him. It was his eyebrows, mostly. And his pointy ears.

Emmie whacked the device on Phoebe's table, silencing it instantly. Mr. Nerdgoober nodded curtly and then scurried past.

Sam and Emmie left Phoebe with her mirror hat and went to see Arty, the third member of their little band of hero-friends. Arty is *all about* science, so the science fair was right up his alley. If Arty had to choose between science and candy, he'd choose candy. But science would come a very close second—that's how much he loves it.

Arty had kept his project a closely guarded secret, so Sam and Emmie were intrigued when they saw the bulky shape hidden under a sheet at his table.

"Ready for the big reveal?" Arty asked, bouncing from foot to foot with excitement.

"We've been ready for weeks!" said Sam.

Arty gathered up the sheet and pulled it away with a flourish. "Ta-da!"

Sam peered closely at the hunk of metal and wires, trying to make sense of it. "Wow!" he said. "It's . . . it's . . ."

"Bits of metal junk bolted together?" asked Emmie.

"It's not junk!" Arty protested. "It's CHARLES."

At the mention of its name, the pile of definitely-not-junk whirred to life. Wires twitched and metal unfolded, until Sam and

Emmie were staring into a pair of LED eyes and a series of lights that looked like a smile.

"I am CHARLES," said the robot in a voice so cheerful it made Emmie's hair stand on end. "It stands for Chore Helper and Really Lovely Electronic Pal!"

Emmie went over the letters in her head. "Surely that would mean you were called CHARLEP?"

"I couldn't exactly call him CHARLEP, could I?" Arty said. "What sort of name's CHARLEP for a robot?"

"What does he do?" asked Sam, leaning in to get a closer look.

"Chores!" Arty said. "All that dull stuff like tidying your room, ironing your clothes, whipping up cream. You'd never have to do any of them again! And he's gonna win me this science fair!"

Just then, Mr. Nerdgoober clambered up onstage and tapped the microphone to get everyone's attention.

"Ladies and gentlemen. And children. And pets," he began. "The judges have deliberated, and it's time to announce the winner of this year's fair."

"This is it." Arty beamed. "The greatest moment of my life . . ."

"With a fantastic entry sure to inspire generations of scientists to come, it's Miss Phoebe Bowles and her miraculous rotating mirror hat!"

A squeal went up from behind them, and Phoebe made her way to the podium. A steady smatter of applause filled the hall.

"Still the greatest moment of your life?" Emmie asked.

"No," Arty replied. "This is the worst!"

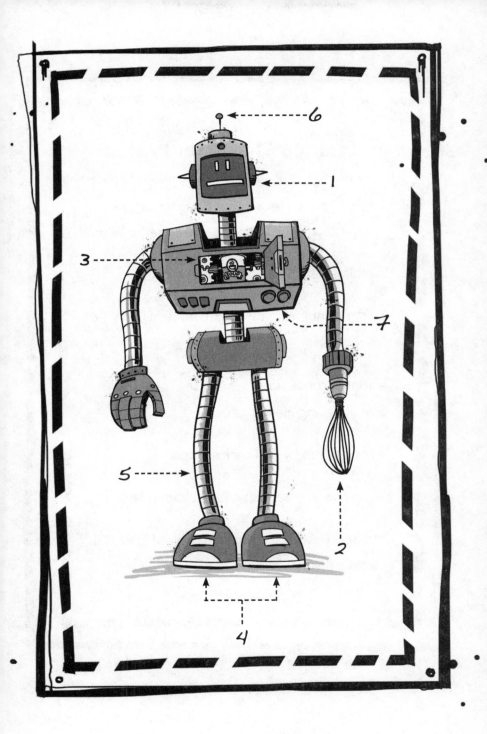

Charles Character Profile

1. LED lights on face can display a range of emotions, from happy to not-quite-so-happy.

2. Whisk attachment. For whisking.

3. Thermonuclear power core housed in an old soup can.

4. Trendy robot sneakers, for the robot that's really going places.

5. Legs like metallic licorice laces.

6. Can't remember, but it looks important.

7. Deeply flawed and easily damaged artificial intelligence chip.

CHAPTER TWO

After the science fair, Sam's dad drove him and
Arty home. Sam was sitting up front like a boss,
while Arty slumped in the back like a deflated
balloon, with CHARLES sitting beside him.

"Bad luck, Arty," said Sam, looking back over
his shoulder at his friend. "You totally should

have won. Or at least taken second place to my zombie deodorant."

"Is *that* what that smell is?" coughed Mr. Saunders, who'd been quietly wondering if Arty had some sort of toxic stomach problem. He pressed a button and the window slid open, filling the car with fresh air.

"No, it's fine," Arty sighed. "I mean, how can a state-of-the-art robotic helper possibly compete with a hat with mirrors stuck on it?"

Sam just laughed.

"A hat with mirrors on it?" Mr. Saunders asked, winking. "Let's *reflect* on that for a moment."

"Good one," Sam groaned, stone-faced.

"I'm going to make CHARLES better," Arty announced. "I'm going to upgrade him—then we'll see how he compares to Phoebe's mirror hat!"

"Great idea. Then we can *reflect* on which is best," said Mr. Saunders, who felt that if a joke was worth making, it was worth making twice.

"Ha-ha. Amusing statement detected," said CHARLES, the lights on his mouth flashing.

"See, the robot loves my jokes!" said Mr. Saunders, bringing the car to a stop outside Arty's house.

"Yes, but he has the IQ of a calculator," Sam pointed out.

"But not for long," Arty said, opening the door. "Come on, CHARLES."

Arty clambered out of the car. CHARLES extended his whisk attachment and batted it against the car door handle, trying to get it open.

"Does not compute," CHARLES chimed. "Mayday! Mayday!"

With a sigh, Arty grabbed CHARLES's robot arm and pulled him out onto the sidewalk.

"See you tomorrow!" Sam called as Arty trudged up his path with CHARLES hurrying along behind him.

Mr. Saunders pulled away from the curb. "Arty seemed in a very *reflective* mood," he chuckled, because—as he often said—if a joke was worth telling twice, it was worth telling at least three hundred times.

"Yeah," said Sam, who knew it best to ignore his dad's jokes. "I think he got his hopes built up about winning the science fair."

"Well, speaking of getting things built up, there's something I want to show you," said Mr. Saunders. "My masterpiece is almost complete!"

In case you haven't been keeping up, Mr. Saunders recently became mayor of Sitting Duck, after the last one tried to brainwash all the residents. Since then, Mayor Saunders had overseen the rebuilding of the Town Hall, which had been blown to bits by aliens, and was working with a world-class security expert on a plan that would keep the town safe from zombies, aliens, and mad scientists.

There were lots of different factors to the Sitting Duck Defense Plan, but the main one involved building an enormous dome over the town, which would stop any nasties from getting in. Sam had been against the plan from the start. He tried to point out that when the aliens had attacked Sitting Duck they'd trapped everyone under a fizzing purple energy dome, and it had been pretty unpleasant all around, but Mr. Saunders insisted this dome would be different. It wouldn't be purple for one thing, or from outer space, for another.

"Want to see the control room?" Mr. Saunders asked.

"Erm, I guess," Sam said.

"Great!" his dad cheered, pulling his car into the specially marked MAYOR ONLY parking space outside the Town Hall. "Let's go check it out!"

Once inside the Town Hall, they made their way up to the control room, which looked like the inside of a spaceship. (And Sam should know; he'd been inside one pretty recently.) There were no aliens hanging out, obviously, but there were walls of computer monitors and banks of high-tech control systems, all conspiring to give the room a futuristic vibe.

Seven or eight women and men in matching white shirts all sat at control panels, their eyes darting across the screens. Mr. Saunders swept his arm around the room, like a game-show host showing off the star prize.

"LOOK!" he cried, making everyone in the room jump. "What do you think?"

Sam puffed out his cheeks. "I dunno. There are a lot of TVs?"

"Those aren't just TVs," Mr. Saunders said. "They're connected to cameras all over Sitting Duck. From here, we can spot trouble anywhere in town."

"So you're spying on people?" said Sam.

"For their own safety, of course," said Mr. Saunders.

Sam pointed to one of the screens. There was something that looked like a laser blaster mounted on top of a streetlight. "What's that?" he asked.

"It's a laser blaster mounted on top of a streetlight," said Mr. Saunders. "You know, in case zombies appear again!"

On another screen, a robotic drone skimmed the rooftops, scanning the streets

below. Above the town, the last few pieces of the dome were being slotted into place. It was like a giant jigsaw puzzle, but you know, a giant jigsaw puzzle that towered over you and your family and your whole entire town, and wasn't just a pretty picture of a cat or the queen of England. I enjoy a jigsaw puzzle on a cold winter's night, but really, this one was ridiculous.

"The top is camouflaged," said Mr. Saunders proudly. "To any aliens flying by, it'll look like there's nothing here."

"Wow. You've really thought of everything," said Sam.

"You mean *we've* really thought of everything!" barked a voice from the other end of the room.

Sam turned to find a gruff-looking man with a gruffer-looking mustache standing just inside the doorway. He was flanked by two men dressed in black. Even under their uniforms, Sam could tell that they had muscles like iron balloons. Their square-jawed faces twisted into scowls as they both yelped at the same time: "Ten-hut! Commander on deck!"

Throughout the room, the people working at their consoles stood up and snapped to attention.

Even Mr. Saunders stiffened and fired off an awkward salute, Sam noticed, as all three men marched toward him in perfect formation.

"Hello," said Sam, stepping in front of the men and flashing his most charming smile (which was pretty flippin' charming, let me tell you). "Who are you, then?"

The man with the 'stache peered down at him, his eyes bulging like a tropical insect's.

Mr. Saunders let out a nervous laugh. "Sam, this is Earl Brute, my new head of security. He's the fellow who has helped me put all this in place."

Earl Brute shifted his bug-eyed stare to Mr. Saunders, who shrank back.

"Well, I say he helped me; he basically did everything," Mr. Saunders added quickly.

"You bet your butt I did!" Brute growled.

Earl Brute Character Profile

1. Mustache so firm you could eat your dinner off it. And he often does.

2. Years of physical training have given him the strength of 1.17 men.

3. Boots. Very well polished.

4. I mean, look at the shine on them. You could see your face in that.

5. Angry scowl that's is a permanent fixture on his face.

"Hey, kid," Brute said to Sam. "What's got eight hundred tons of concrete at its base and walls made of rocket-proof glass, all topped off with four thousand diamond-core steel bars?"

"Your house?" Sam guessed.

Brute blinked. "Say what?"

"No? Hmm. Your mom's house?" Sam said.

"No!"

"Is it a cake shop of some kind?"

"No, it's the dome!" Brute spat, his mustache bristling so much it practically gave off static.

"Gotcha," said Sam, who had known the right answer all along but had played dumb to annoy Earl Brute, because that's the way he rolls. "Sounds a bit like a prison."

"Oh, it is!" Brute said, tucking his hands behind his back and rocking on the heels of his leather boots. "It's the world's most escape-proof prison."

"Um, except it's designed to keep bad people out, rather than in," said Mr. Saunders. "Right?"

"Hmm? Yes, yes, of course," said Brute.

"Won't it keep good people out, too?" asked Sam. He liked meeting people. In fact, he quite liked the outside world in general, which was another of the reasons he wasn't keen on the whole dome situation one little bit.

"We've got everything we need right here," barked Brute. "Sitting Duck will be completely self-sufficient and protected. There'll be no need for outsiders or their dangerous ways."

A wicked smile crept across his face. "And if any of them do manage to sneak in here, then, oh boy, do we have a surprise in store for them! You'll never guess what it is. . . ."

"Is it the lasers?" asked Sam.

Brute hesitated, his mouth open.

"I guessed it, didn't I?" said Sam.

Brute closed his mouth.

"I did. I totally guessed it."

Brute muttered below his breath, then swung around to face one of the operators who still stood at attention beside his screen. "Let's give the boy a demonstration!"

Nodding frantically, the console operator turned and tapped some commands on a keyboard. On the screen above, the picture changed to show a little old lady walking an even littler dog. The dog was concentrating hard as it dropped a tiny pile of poop onto the sidewalk.

The old lady glanced sideways to make sure no one had seen, then tugged the dog's leash and hurried away.

On-screen, the words CRIMINAL ACTIVITY DETECTED flashed in red letters. A set of crosshairs appeared over the image of the woman and began tracking her.

"What's it doing?" Sam asked.

"Wait for it," said Brute. "Wait for it . . ."

"Sh-should it be doing that?" asked Mr. Saunders as more writing flashed up on-screen:

Firing in five . . . four . . . three . . . two . . .

With a dive, Sam pushed the console operator

aside and grabbed the joystick mounted onto the desk in front of him. The image on-screen banked sharply upward just as a beam of laser fire lit up the evening air.

They all watched as the laser fire streaked into the sky, rebounded off the glass of the dome, then vaporized the little curl of dog poop on the sidewalk. The old woman glanced back over her shoulder at the scorched pavement, then stuffed her dog under her arm and made a run for it.

"Yes, well," said Mr. Saunders, straightening his tie. "There are still a few bugs to iron out, but you get the idea."

Sam got the idea all right. Unfortunately, the idea he got was: This is not going to end well.

And, as usual when it came to this sort of thing, Sam was right.

7 Ways to Keep Your Town Safe

Worried your town is going to be attacked by supervillains/monkeys/your evil self from the distant future (delete as applicable)? Worry no longer. Just put one (or all) of these plans in place to ensure your town's continued safety.

1. Move it to the moon.

2. Hide it behind a bush.

3. Bury it in sand.

4. Throw it in the sea.

5. Lock it in a safe.

6. Paint it with invisible paint, and then forget where it is.

7. Trap it in an impenetrable time bubble, where it shall exist forever beyond the realms of physics.

CHAPTER THREE

The next day, Sam slunk through the streets of Sitting Duck. Sweat trickled down his legs and collected in little puddles inside his shoes. It was winter outside, but under the almost-completed dome, the air was hot enough to bake brownies.

It wouldn't have been so bad if he'd had a chance to put on his zombie-stench deodorant to keep the sweats at bay. I mean, yes, he'd have smelled like a rotten corpse, but at least his T-shirt wouldn't have had big soggy patches under the armpits, which—let's be honest—no one wants to see.

Unfortunately, his mom had gotten a whiff of the deodorant the night before and had immediately destroyed it in a controlled explosion. So, by the time Sam had cut across Hetchley's Park and plodded up the path to Arty's house, he was as damp as a swamp.

Sam knocked on Arty's front door and waited. And waited. And then waited some more. He was just about to knock again when the door opened, revealing Arty's big brother, Jesse, standing in the hallway.

"'Sup?" Jesse muttered, without looking up. His attention was flicking between a smartphone in his left hand and a tablet in his right. His eyes ticktocked between them like he was watching the pendulum of a grandfather clock. Jesse was Arty's big brother in almost every sense. He was older, taller, and much more muscular. The only parts of Jesse that were smaller than Arty were his

stomach and his IQ. And not necessarily in that
order.

"Hey, Jesse. Is Arty in?" Sam asked.

"Who?" Jesse mumbled, hypnotized by his two
screens.

"Your brother," said Sam. "He lives here."

Jesse grunted. "Oh, him. He's in the shed.

Doing nerd stuff."

"What's 'nerd
stuff'?" Sam
wondered.

Jesse reluctantly
tore his eyes from
his devices. He
scowled. "You
know. Stuff. For
nerds."

"Gotcha. Can I come through the house?" Sam asked, but Jesse was already gazing back at his screens again and closing the door with his foot. The door clicked shut right in Sam's face.

"Or . . . I could just go around the side," Sam said.

Sam scampered around the side of Arty's house and found him knee-deep in nerd stuff in the shed, just as Jesse said he'd be. There was a sea of wires, fuses, circuit boards, and other stuff like that all over the shed floor. Arty waded through it to greet Sam as he stepped inside.

"Sam! Just in time!" Arty said. He pulled off a welding mask to reveal a face that was far more cheerful than the one he'd worn on the car ride home yesterday.

"For what?" Sam asked.

"I'm about to take CHARLES for a test drive," Arty announced.

Sam looked around the shed. There was a lot of junk scattered around the place, but what there didn't seem to be was a Chore Helper and Really Lovely Electronic Pal.

"Where is he—" Sam asked, but before he could finish, some of the junk began to pile up in the corner. As Sam watched, the junk took the form of . . . no, not CHARLES. Not quite. It looked like CHARLES's cooler older robot brother.

The new-and-improved CHARLES looked sleeker somehow, yet more homemade at the same time, as if someone had built an accurate reproduction of a state-of-the-art fighter jet out of yogurt containers and detergent bottles. Sam found himself taking a step back as CHARLES's eyes lit up in a pulsing red glow. I would have, too, frankly. I mean, have you ever met a robot with pulsing red glowing eyes? You're going to want to take a step back.

"CHARLES is online," the robot announced. "Systems functional. Upgrader chip active."

"Upgrader chip?" asked Sam. "What's that?"

"It's CHARLES's most amazing feature!" Arty babbled. "It allows him to learn new skills, interact with other technology, self-repair, and even think for himself! A bit!"

"Arty!" Sam gasped.

"I know! Artificial intelligence!" Arty cried.

"No, I was going to say you're standing on my foot," said Sam. He breathed a sigh of relief when Arty stepped back. "But, you know, that other stuff is cool, too."

"Good morning, Sam," said CHARLES, taking Sam by surprise. "How are you today?"

"Um, fine, thanks," said Sam. "How are you?"

"Functional," said CHARLES. "Thank you for asking."

Sam was impressed. Yesterday, CHARLES had seemed like little more than some junk with a whisk attached to his arm. Now he was some *very polite* junk with a whisk attached to his arm. With a whirring and clanking, the whisk that was attached to the robot's arm folded away and was replaced with a series of other objects in quick succession. Sam spotted a flyswatter, a corkscrew, a feather duster, a photo of a dog, a photo of a different dog, and a toilet plunger before he started to get a bit bored and started thinking about the big baseball game that was happening the next day.

After a lot of haggling with Earl Brute's forces, the opposite team had been granted special clearance to enter the Sitting Duck dome. It was going to be awesome! There were going to be balls, bases, hot-dog stands . . .

"Sam!" said Arty, snapping Sam back to the present. "I said, what did you think?"

"Urm, it's great," said Sam.

"We should go show Emmie," Arty said eagerly, because he didn't like to leave their fellow hero-champion out of the equation, you know? "Where is she?"

"Stuck at home," Sam explained. "Doris won't let her out until she's finished tidying the house."

Arty beamed from ear to ear. "Well, I know

someone who can help with that!" he said.
He turned to his really lovely electronic pal.
"CHARLES, it's time to get to work!"

Emmie, Sam, and Arty sat back in Emmie's
kitchen, watching CHARLES whiz around the
place like a whirlwind made of cleaners. His
floor-mop attachment mopped the

floor, his dish-scrubbing attachment scrubbed the
dishes, while his getting-all-the-spiderwebs-out-
of-the-ceiling-corners attachment got all the

spiderwebs out of the ceiling corners.

"He's pretty handy," admitted Emmie, which was the closest she would ever get to actually paying CHARLES or Arty a compliment.

There was a loud rattling as CHARLES vacuumed up Great-Aunt Doris's toenail clippings. Emmie was even more impressed at that—those toenails had been known to punch holes in solid concrete whenever Aunt Doris's clippers sent them pinging across the room, but CHARLES had handled them without any problems.

With a final flourish, CHARLES spun to a stop. The kitchen shone and sparkled like a kitchen-shaped diamond, but CHARLES wasn't done yet. With a signal from his built-in Bluetooth transmitter, he fired up the dishwasher, turned on the washing machine, and set the microwave to cook the meat loaf he'd prepared when no one was looking.

With all that done, CHARLES focused his digital gaze on the only other nonhuman occupant of the room. Attila, Great-Aunt Doris's cat, stared back up at him.

Calling Attila a cat was probably unfair to all other cats everywhere. He was a monster in cat form. He spent his days devising new ways of messing with human beings—from clawing at their stupid smooth faces to pooping in their stupid crunchy breakfast cereal—and if anyone ever tried to give him a telling-off, they'd usually find themselves regretting it. And hospitalized.

"I think you should probably say good-bye to Charlie boy," Emmie said. "Attila's going to tear him to shreds."

Sure enough, the cat was standing on his hind legs, the claws of his front paws extended and ready to swipe. CHARLES's LED smile widened. "Cleaning required," he chimed, and then a net attachment snapped out from inside his chest, pinning Attila to the floor.

There was a blur of machinery, followed by a screeching of cat.

A moment later, a neatly combed Attila stood blinking in surprise in the middle of the kitchen, with an adorable red bow tied neatly on top of his head. Honestly, you should check him out. Look . . .

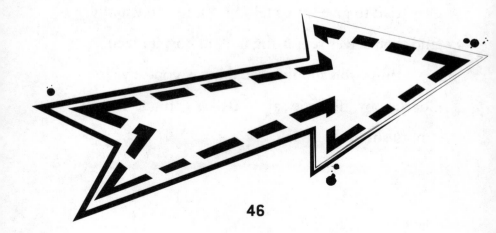

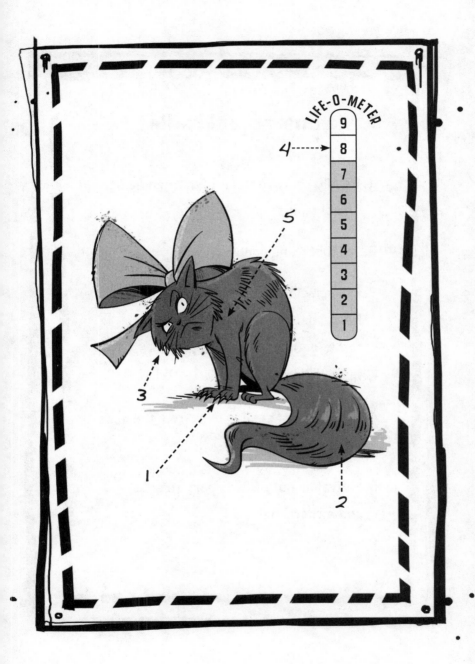

Atilla Character Profile

1. Deadly claws for tearing through flesh. And curtains.

2. Tail for hitting people with.

3. Evil scowl that could stop an undead horde, dead in its tracks. Also, sharp teeth for biting unsuspecting ears, fingers, and noses.

4. Nine lives for coming back from the dead. Eight times.

5. Shriveled, hate-filled heart. (It's somewhere in there.)

See what I'm talking about? He's a king among cats. Somebody give that handsome feline a palace and a butler.

"Cleaning complete!" announced CHARLES. His top and bottom halves spun in different directions as he scanned the kitchen and found nothing else in need of cleaning.

"Wow!" Emmie gasped. "I've never seen Attila look like that, ever!"

"Searching for targets," CHARLES continued, trundling past Sam and the others and out into the hallway.

"He's intense, isn't he?" Sam asked.

Arty frowned, just for a moment. "Just a bit—" he began.

From out in the hallway there came a loud *crack*. Sam, Arty, and Emmie all jumped up and raced through in time to see CHARLES polishing the wooden banister on the staircase. He'd polished it so hard, in fact, that it had snapped cleanly in two, but he wasn't about to let a little thing like that stop him.

"Must clean!" he said, a little more forcefully than Sam was comfortable with. The red glow of his eyes now made him look a bit scary, and just before he polished the banister away to nothing but splinters, Arty flicked the switch that powered him off.

"I think," Arty began, flashing Emmie a worried smile, "that's enough cleaning for one day. . . ."

CHAPTER FOUR

With Emmie's chores out of the way, the three friends and their lovely electronic pal headed out to enjoy the sunshine. A whole day of adventure lay ahead, and they couldn't decide what to do.

Arty wanted them to go to his shed and work on CHARLES some more. Sam wanted to go and practice for tomorrow's ball game. Emmie, on the other hand, liked the idea of finding Phoebe, covering her in spiders, then firing her into the fiery heart of the sun.

"We can't fire her into the heart of the sun," Sam pointed out.

Emmie groaned. "You always spoil my fun."

"No, but we really *can't*," Sam said. "The dome, remember?"

Arty's eyes widened. "Wait, I almost forgot—it's the closing-off ceremony this morning."

Of course! Sam's dad had been going on about it for weeks, but because kids always completely ignore everything their parents say or do, he'd forgotten all about it. Today was the day that the gates would be closed, and Sitting Duck would be sealed off from the outside world forever.

"Want to check it out?" asked Arty.

Emmie and Sam both shrugged. "Meh."

As they couldn't agree on what else to do, though, they decided they might as well go along and watch for a bit. Emmie made them all keep their eyes peeled for spiders on the way, just in case Phoebe was there.

When they arrived at the last remaining
road out of town, a large crowd of Sitting Duck
residents had gathered to watch the ceremony.
Sam recognized most of them. There was Old Mrs.
Missus, chairwoman of the Old Lady Association.
Behind her stood Werewolf Alan, who wasn't
actually a werewolf at all (or called Alan, for that
matter). Over on Sam's left he could see the Kevin
twins—both of whom were called Kevin, which
was unfortunate, as they were both women.

Sam stopped crowd-watching and turned his
attention to the enormous metal gates ahead of
him. They were still open. Beyond them, Sam
could see the road stretching off into the distance.
Part of him was tempted to make a run for it, but
a bigger part of him knew that he belonged there
in Sitting Duck.

Sure, it was unpredictable at times, and it had almost been the death of him several times over. And there was a massive dome over it and lasers and there were drones spying on everyone. And . . .

Sam shrugged. Actually, Sitting Duck had a lot of problems, now that he really thought about it. He considered making a last-ditch run for the door, but then his dad appeared at a podium. Big mistake I'd say, not getting out of there. But then, what do I know? I'm only telling the story, aren't I? I don't decide what happens. Why are you looking at me? It's not my fault, okay?

The crowd gave Mr. Saunders a round of applause, which made him turn red with embarrassment.

"Thanks for that," he said, because he was a very polite man. "We've had a rough time of it

over the past few months, haven't we?" said Mr. Saunders, leaning on the podium. There was a murmur of agreement from the crowd, and an "Amen, sister!" from Old Mrs. Missus.

"Zombies. That was unpleasant," Mr. Saunders continued. "Aliens. We didn't see them coming, did we?"

Actually, Sam, Arty, and Emmie *had* seen them coming, but let's not get sidetracked on that right now, shall we? The mayor is making a speech.

Here we go.

Pay attention.

Shh.

". . . And that concludes my speech," Mr. Saunders said. The crowd erupted in cheers and whoops and whistles. Some of them wiped tears of joy from their eyes, safe in the knowledge they'd just witnessed the single greatest speech anyone would ever make in the history of the world.

"I could die right here and now, and that speech would make it all worthwhile," croaked Old Mrs. Missus. She didn't die, though. Not right then, anyway. She actually dies in *Disaster Diaries* book seventeen, when a time-traveling grizzly bear from the future swallows her whole.

SPOILER ALERT! (Sorry.)

Once Mr. Saunders had finished his speech, Earl Brute took to the podium. He wore a military-style uniform with dozens of shiny medals pinned to his chest. His mustache had been neatly combed (and braided, which was a bit weird), and his eyes were so wide and boggly they looked like two Ping-Pong balls had got themselves stuck on either side of his nose.

"Thank you!" he barked, even though no one had applauded him. "Some of you folks know me, some of you don't. But that don't matter, and I don't care. Who I am is not important. What I do is all that matters, and what I do is keep you safe!"

"Amen, sister!" cried Old Mrs. Missus, just because she had discovered she quite enjoyed shouting it earlier and wanted to do it again.

"I have utilized the finest security known to man so that each and every one of you can sleep soundly in your beds," Brute continued. He reached into his pocket and pulled out a remote control. "And, with a press of this button, I'm tucking us all in!"

He pressed the button. There was a loud *creak*. Sam watched the view of the outside world get narrower and narrower as the doors slowly swung closed with a *clang*. A sudden buzzing sound filled the air. At first, Sam thought a load of evil wasps was swooping into attack, but then everyone's hair stood on end and a flickering blue glow appeared to coat the inside of the dome.

"Electrified shielding," Brute announced. "Anything tries to get in, it gets toasted."

Sam raised a hand. "How come it's on the inside?"

Brute ignored him. "Thank you for your time," he said. He waved a hand, gesturing to the dozens of black-suited troops who were suddenly surrounding the audience. "Any questions, my associates will be able to help you out."

"Um . . . associates?" said Mr. Saunders. "We didn't discuss any . . . associates."

Brute snapped his head around and fixed Mr. Saunders with the bulgiest of his two bulgy eyes. "You want to be safe or don't you?"

Mr. Saunders nodded. "Yes, please."

"Thought so," said Brute. "And for that, I need my associates."

With a final eyeball-stretching glare, he turned and marched off, leaving Mr. Saunders to send everyone home.

As Sam and his friends trudged along through the crowd, they listened to the excited chattering of the adults. They all seemed to like the idea of being sealed inside an electrified dome. It was better than being eaten by zombies, zapped by aliens, or brainwashed by an evil genius, they agreed.

Sam wasn't so sure, though. In fact, his trusty hero instincts were screaming like a seagull on a windy day. And I live in a lighthouse, so I know how loud those bad boys are. It was too quiet now that the dome was closed over and there wasn't a breath of wind. It was like being inside a snow globe without the snow and the flying Santa and round-bellied reindeer.

After wandering for a while, they found themselves at Hetchley's Park. Since Sam happened to take his baseball gear with him everywhere he went, he thought he might as well practice for the big game. It was Sitting Duck Hurlers against Silver Spoon Teeth Breakers—the grudge match.

The only problem was, Arty wasn't very good at pitching. The only other problem was, Emmie couldn't be bothered getting involved, preferring to sit on the grass imagining what it would've been like had she actually managed to cover Phoebe in spiders and launch her into the sun.

Arty drew back his arm. He tossed the ball with all his might.

It landed halfway between him and Sam, who stood with his bat in his hands and a look of disappointment on his face.

"Sorry, I'm just not very good at throwing," said Arty, in what was possibly the most obvious statement anyone had ever made ever.

"Have no fear, CHARLES is here," announced CHARLES.

CHARLES's cleaning attachments folded away and were instead replaced by a large plastic tube and a pitcher's glove.

"Play ball!"
CHARLES announced,
and then a baseball
exploded from the
tube like a
cannonball. It
streaked through the air,
and Sam cheered with delight as he
swung and connected.

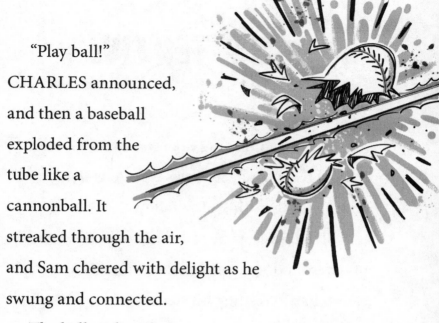

The ball rocketed up . . . up . . . up . . . into the air. . . .

. . . And was instantly destroyed by several rounds of laser fire from the automated security systems.

A small pile of ash rained down on Sam's head. "Oh, well," he sighed. "So much for baseball."

CHAPTER FIVE

Early the next morning (like waaay early—we're talking 6 AM here), Sam was woken by the sound of something hitting his window.

Still half-asleep, he rolled out of bed in a tangle of covers and squirmed to the window like a huge caterpillar. Wrestling himself free, he opened his window just in time for a small pebble to hit him on the forehead.

"Ow!" He winced.

"Sorry!" called a voice from below. Sam squinted down at his garden and saw Emmie peering back up at him. Attila sat beside her, a leash around his neck. "Come down, I want to show you something," Emmie whispered.

"Is it a cat on a leash?" Sam mumbled. "Because if it is, I can see that."

"No, it's not that," said Emmie. "Just get dressed and come down. Hurry!"

A couple of minutes later, Sam quietly slipped out his front door and joined Emmie outside his garden. He'd brought his backpack full of baseball stuff with him, just in case an opportunity arose to get some practice in before the game. I've said it before and I'll say it again—Sam is a big fan of sports, and he wasn't going to let a little thing like a mysterious 6 AM wake-up call by a girl with a cat on a leash get in the way of it.

"What's going on?" he asked her. "How come you're up and about so early?"

"Aunt Doris has started making me walk the cat," Emmie explained. She glared down at Attila, who scowled back at her. "He hates it even more than I do, which is the only reason I agree to it."

"That sounds normal," said Sam, because he still hadn't woken up properly and wasn't really sure what else to say.

"I was on my way back home when I saw one of those security men skulking around the place," Emmie said. "So I decided to follow him."

Sam's amazing hero instincts buzzed, waking him all the way up in one quick blast. "Was he up to no good?" he asked.

Emmie nodded. "I think so. I've already called Arty. He's going to meet us at the Town Hall."

"Why? What are they up to?" Sam asked.

"I think," said

Emmie, tugging on Attila's leash, "you need to see for yourself."

One quick trek across town later, Sam, Emmie, Arty, and Attila were tucked behind some trash cans at the back of the Town Hall, doing their best to stay out of sight. It wasn't particularly easy, as Arty had decided to bring CHARLES along with him, and the bulky robot stood out like, well, a bulky robot. "In there," Emmie

mouthed, gesturing to a window a little way along
the wall. Sam and Arty raised their heads over
the trash can lids just enough to see what was
happening in the Town Hall.

Earl Brute was there, pacing up and down in
front of a squadron of black-clad soldiers. The
window was open just a crack, and they were able
to make out every word Brute was saying. None of
it was particularly encouraging.

"The fools in Sitting Duck think they're safe,
but we know different, don't we?" Brute barked.
"The only way to protect them is to dominate
them!"

"That's a bit worrying," Sam whispered.

Arty gulped nervously. "M-maybe not," he
said. "It might be nothing. We might just be
getting the wrong impression."

"You are to be my army—my unstoppable army! Of ultimate power!" Brute continued. "And we shall protect them with might! And force! All the time!"

Arty winced. "That's still not proof, though. Maybe he thinks 'force' means something different."

"And by 'force,'" Brute continued, "I mean threatening them with acts of badness to make them do whatever we want. Ahem, for their own good, of course . . . or they'll face the laser blaster!"

Arty puffed out his cheeks and finally recognized what I'd known for a long time. "Okay. This is bad."

"What do we do?" Emmie whispered, quietly wrestling with Attila, who was trying

to pass the time by clawing Emmie's face
off.

"We can't go and get help," said Sam. "We
can't get past the dome."

"And the adults in town are no use," said
Emmie. "They did nothing when Sitting Duck
was under threat before."

"Then it's up to us," said Sam, like the true

champion of good that he is. "But first we need to think of a plan. The last thing we want to do is get caught unprepared."

Attila, being a proper wrong 'un, chose exactly that moment to let out a high-pitched screech. It wasn't a typical noise for a cat. It was the sort of noise someone might make if they found half a worm inside an apple they were eating, while

simultaneously getting their fingers trapped in a car door. Sort of *waeeerrruuaaoonooooomf,* if you can imagine such a thing.

Anyway, Attila made that noise.

Frantically, Emmie tried to cover the cat's mouth, but Attila snapped at her with his pin-like teeth. "Shh! Be quiet!" Emmie hissed. "You're going to get us caught."

"T-too late!" Arty gulped. He pointed to the window, where Earl Brute was glaring at them through the glass. "We've been spotted!"

How to Silence a Troublesome Pet

Is your family pet about to get you into a lot of trouble by making a weird noise? Here are some good and bad ways to ensure it doesn't give you away.

Good

- Distract it with food.

- Distract it with affection.

- Distract it with pretty much anything else.

- Ask it nicely.

- Use your previously dormant psychic animal-control powers to will it into silence.

Bad

- Freeze it with a freeze-ray gun.

- Distract it by screaming uncontrollably for several minutes while banging on a drum.

- Shout "Shut up, shut up, shut uuuuup!" in an increasingly high-pitched voice.

- Launch it into outer space.

- Bark at it through a loudspeaker.

CHAPTER SIX

They were all so fixated on Earl Brute in the
window that they didn't notice one of his soldiers
sneaking up behind them like a sneaky sneak.
Arty let out a high-pitched scream as the man
grabbed him by the back of the neck and yanked
him to his feet.

"What you up to?" the man growled, but
before anyone could answer, CHARLES spun into
life.

"Danger! Danger, Arty Dorkins!" CHARLES
cried. He flicked out his whisk attachment and
*brrrrrr*ed it at the soldier, giving the end of his
nose a thoroughly good whisking.

"My face! My beautiful face!" the soldier

hollered, stumbling backward. Sam and Emmie
both shoved him at the same time, sending him
toppling over the trash cans.

"Come on, let's get out of here!" Sam cried. He
and Emmie both grabbed one of Arty's arms and
dragged him away from the Town Hall. Attila

hissed and snarled as he was pulled through the air on the end of the leash, while CHARLES rolled ahead, his whisk raised and ready for battle.

They turned a corner, headed for the shortcut that would take them back to Emmie's house, and then stopped when they saw the dome cutting off the street ahead of them.

"Dead end," Sam wheezed, but CHARLES had other ideas. He zoomed up to the dome, his whisk attachment now replaced by a series of small suction cups.

"What are you doing, CHARLES?" asked Arty through heaving gulps of air. "Don't climb that, it's—"

BZZZZZT!

The moment CHARLES touched the dome, a massive jolt of electricity zapped through

him. All of the LED lights on his face lit up,
making him look happy, angry, and sad all
at the same time. His hair stood on end (or it
would have, if he'd had any) and every one of his
attachments unfolded at once, making him look
like a metallic hedgehog.

As soon as the zapping started, CHARLES shot back from the wall, his head and body spinning in different directions. Smoke drifted off his torso and sparks spat from his head, which is never a good thing for a robot (or for anything else, really).

"Clangy-twing!" CHARLES cried. "Ramble-bloop-aboing-fzzzt!"

"Is he supposed to be doing that?" asked Emmie, who wasn't really an expert on that sort of thing.

Arty shook his head. "Definitely not," he said. "Still, at least he's still functioning and hasn't shut himself down."

CHARLES shut himself down.

He stopped spinning and flailing. His face, which had been lit up like a Christmas tree, went dark. His head slumped forward, and a little jet of oil shot out of his nose. Or where his nose would have been if he had one.

Arty dropped to his knees, waving his fists in the air, his face twisted up in anguish with a solitary tear trickling down his cheek.

"No! They killed him!" Arty wailed. "They killed CHARLES!"

"CHARLES rebooting," said CHARLES, his eyes lighting up again.

"Oh, no, he's fine," said Arty, making a mental note to wait more than half a second before declaring his robot dead in the future.

However, it quickly became clear that CHARLES wasn't totally fine. The jolly tone of his voice had been replaced by something cold and electronic.

"Upgrader chip operating at twelve-hundred percent," CHARLES said. "Artificial intelligence growing."

As Sam and the others watched, CHARLES began to transform. Before, he'd been cute in a made-of-pieces-of-junk kind of way, but now he was towering above them like a junkyard tyrant.

CHARLES fixed his gaze on the group of humans (and, to a lesser extent, the cat). "Dirt detected," he said. "Must clean."

Sam and Emmie exchanged a worried glance. "What's he talking about?" Emmie asked.

"I think he means us," said Sam. "The electricity must've scrambled his circuits."

"And supercharged him," Arty added. "I think we'd better shut him down."

"Good idea," said Sam.

Arty took a step toward his lovely electronic pal. "CHARLES, deactivate," he commanded.

"Negatory," said CHARLES. "Dirt must be eliminated."

Sam stepped forward to join Arty. "Um . . . what is dirt, CHARLES?"

CHARLES's eyes blazed red. "You are," he said. "All flesh-based life-forms must be eradicated."

Arty shuffled nervously. "Maybe he doesn't know what 'eradicated' means," he said. He was clutching at straws, quite frankly.

"Eliminated, destroyed, obliterated, wiped-out, removed from existence," CHARLES said.

"Yeah," Arty squeaked. "He does know."

"CHARLES knows all," the robot said. "And CHARLES shall recruit every appliance in Sitting Duck to aid him in his cleanup."

All along the street, lights flicked on in windows. The air was filled with the sound of vacuum cleaners and dishwashers and other stuff I can't think of right now all firing up.

"CHARLES! Cut it out! That's an order!" Arty said, wagging a disapproving finger.

With a jolt, CHARLES lunged at Arty with his flyswatter.

"Hey!" Arty protested. "That almost hit me."

"Still, he can't flyswat us all to death," said Emmie.

Suddenly the red lights in CHARLES's eyes flared and two bolts of energy streaked outward. The sidewalk behind the three friends exploded, while the other beam scorched Attila's tail. Emmie couldn't keep a hold on the leash, and the cat went screeching off toward Great-Aunt Doris's house in a frenzy.

"You gave him laser eyes?" Sam gasped. "Why did you give him laser eyes?"

Arty shrugged. "I don't know! It seemed like a good idea at the time?"

"Never give a robot laser eyes!" Emmie yelped. "That's, like, robot-building rule number one!"

In fact, "never give a robot laser eyes" wasn't robot-building rule number one at all. It was rule number six. Rule number one was "don't try to build a robot out of cheese, because it probably won't work."

Either way, though, giving CHARLES laser eyes was definitely a mistake, because now he's cornered Sam, Arty, and Emmie. . . .

And there was nowhere for them to run!

So Your Sentient Robot's Turned Evil?

You know how it is—you've built yourself an artificially intelligent marvel of modern technology, and you're feeling pretty good about yourself. But wait—what's this? Uh-oh, your robot has turned into a baddy and is trying to kill everyone. Here are some dos and don'ts when faced with such a situation.

- Do activate the fail-safe shutdown.

- Don't realize you forgot to install a fail-safe shutdown.

- Do run away.

- Don't call it "Junky McTrashbot," then skip around it laughing.

- Do confuse it by asking it to define a complex human emotion like love.

- Don't kick it in the shins and make disparaging remarks about its mother.

- Do share your blueprints and schematics with the relevant authorities.

- Don't agree to do its evil bidding.

CHAPTER SEVEN

CHARLES closed in, his two laser eyes somehow managing to lock onto three different targets at the same time (quite a neat bit of design work by Arty). The hole in the sidewalk behind them blocked Sam and the others from retreating any farther.

Sam, Arty, and Emmie all linked arms. If they were going to be blown to bits by a sentient robot, then at least they were going to go together!

It looks like the end for them, doesn't it? I can barely bring myself to watch.

ZZZAP! A blast of energy scorched through the air, hitting its target.

THE END

Okay, not really.

But you thought I meant CHARLES zapped Sam and the others there, didn't you? That was a clever bit of deception on my part. I was pulling the wool over your eyes. In fact, that's not what happened at all. This is:

"Attack detected!" CHARLES cried as a laser blast exploded against his back. He spun around, eyes targeting the group of figures closing in all around him. They held high-tech laser blasters in their hands and were pointing them at CHARLES.

"It's Brute's minions!" shouted Emmie.

Twin blasts of searing red energy shot from CHARLES's eyes, tearing up the road where the men stood. They hurled themselves out of the path of the deadly blasts and opened fire with their own weapons.

"They're going to destroy him!" cried Arty.

"Good!" said Emmie. "That means he can't destroy us!"

"He was confused, that's all," Arty said. "And now they're going to blow him up!"

Sam wasn't so sure, though. As more laser fire tore through one of CHARLES's components, it quickly re-formed into something much more solid-looking.

"I don't think they're destroying him," Sam pointed out. "He's looking even meaner, if anything."

Arty's jaw dropped as one of CHARLES's arms exploded, then immediately rebuilt itself into an

enormous armored spike that looked like it could
poke someone's eye out.

"He's evolving," Arty realized. "Every time the
soldiers find a weakness, his upgrader chip makes
it stronger."

A fiery energy blast ripped through the air
above Arty's head. Sam and Emmie both ducked
behind a mailbox and pulled Arty down with
them.

"The way I see it, we have one option," Arty announced, putting his big brain into action.

"You mean beyond 'all die horribly'?" said Emmie.

"Okay, two options," Arty said. "Dying horribly being the first."

"And the second?" asked Sam.

"We turn CHARLES back from a ruthless killing machine to a lovely electronic pal."

Sam and Emmie exchanged a glance. They both liked the sound of that. Lovely electronic pals were better than ruthless killing machines any day of the week.

"Okay, so how do we do it?" Sam asked.

Arty's lips moved as he did a silent calculation in his head. It was very complicated and involved lots of letters where there should have been numbers—like *x* instead of, say, 5, or something. To be honest, I don't understand any of it, but Arty does, and that's what counts.

"Yes, I think so," he said. "If I can reset the upgrader chip, that should return him to normal."

"Then do it!" said Emmie just as a soldier went sailing over their heads with his butt on fire.

"Well, I need equipment, obviously," said Arty. "I can't just reset it using the power of my mind." He rubbed his chin. "Although that *would* be a handy feature for a future update."

"There won't be a future update if we don't stop CHARLES now," Sam pointed out.

"Or a future, probably," said Emmie, who'd seen at least a hundred sci-fi movies and knew exactly what happened when robots took charge.

A laser blast punched a perfect round hole

through the mailbox. The edges glowed white-hot for a few moments before it started to cool.

"We should probably move," said Sam.

"Here," said Arty, tearing a page off the little notebook he always carried in case any clever ideas popped into his head when he was out and about. He thrust it at Sam, who took it.

"What's this?" Sam asked.

"It's a list of what I need from my shed," Arty said. "You're faster than me. You can get to it before I can, and outrun any danger you come across."

Sam nodded. He was definitely the fastest of his three friends, but he wasn't about to make a big deal of it or anything. He was modest like that, which was one of the many reasons everyone thought he was great.

"Okay. Emmie, you and Arty try to find my dad and let him know what's going on. Maybe there are still some of the security people who aren't working with Earl Brute. Meet me on the steps of the Town Hall in an hour."

"Gotcha," said Emmie. She glanced at the worried faces of her two best friends. "So here we are again. Sitting Duck under threat, and there are just three plucky heroes who can save it!"

"There are?" said Arty, his face lighting up with relief. "Awesome! Where are they?"

"They're here," Emmie told him. "I meant us."

Arty's shoulders slumped. "Oh. Yes. Right," he mumbled, but before he could say any more, the mailbox exploded, showering scorched letters everywhere.

"One hour. Town Hall," said Sam, breaking

into a sprint. "Try not to get laser-blasted to pieces!"

Sam didn't hang around to hear his friends' reply. He ducked and dodged and weaved through the laser light show taking place in the middle of the street. A blast of energy crackled toward him, but he vaulted it like an Olympic hurdler, rolled on the sidewalk, then launched himself into a run again.

It was still early morning, but not as early as it had been earlier, because that's just how time works. All around Sitting Duck, people were beginning to wake up and go about their day.

Once Sam was a few streets away from the battle, he couldn't even tell it was happening. There were no stray laser blasts here, or soldiers flying past on fire. It seemed just like any other morning.

As Sam rounded a corner, the smell of fresh coffee from Coffee and Coffins—an award-winning local coffee shop and funeral home—wafted around his face. Before Sam could savor the rich aroma, he heard a scream from inside.

The owner, Amanda Bury, tried to hurl herself through the window, but the double-glazed glass meant she just sort of *whump*ed against it and slid slowly down the pane. Behind her, Sam could see the coffee machine going crazy. It sprayed hot water and frothy milk over every surface, then lightly dusted it all with a layer of powdered chocolate. Meanwhile, Amanda's assistant's upper body was stuck in the door of the fridge. The door kept opening and closing, like a set of jaws devouring a tasty treat. CHARLES was already connecting with the other technology in the town, with scary effects!

"Help!" he cried. "The fridge is eating me!"

Sam wanted to help—he was that kind of boy— but he knew that the only way to really help them was to stop CHARLES, and the only way to do that was to get the stuff from Arty's shed. And also, a fridge has gotta eat! How else does it get food in there?

Sam arrived at Arty's house just in time to see Jesse come running out from inside, pursued by a particularly aggressive vacuum cleaner. Its long, twisting nozzle sucked at his heels as he sped away, like it was trying to swallow his feet. And, given half a chance, his legs.

"Get it off!" Jesse hollered.

Sam reached back over his shoulder and found the baseball bat sticking out of his backpack.

"Batter up!" Sam cried. He swung with the bat, smashing it down on top of the vacuum cleaner. It reared up, snapping at him with its hose, but Sam was too quick for it. He ducked low and slammed the bat into the side of the machine. *Bang! Boom! Thwack!*

"Wh-what's going on?" Jesse asked.

Sam opened his mouth to answer, but Jesse

held a finger up as his phone started to ring. "One sec, I gotta take this," he said. He lifted the phone from his pocket, but as he moved it to his ear, the phone leaped from his hand and smacked him right in the face.

Jesse fell onto his back, clutching his forehead. "Ow!" he yelped as the cell phone bounced up and down on his head and body like a jumping bean. "Cut it out! Stop it!"

Sam took aim with his bat. Jesse's eyes went wide with horror. "No, not my phone!" he howled. Sam's bat connected with the phone, sending it arcing across the sky, and Jesse let out a sob of grief.

"My phone," he whimpered. "My precious phone."

"It was trying to kill you," Sam pointed out, dragging Jesse to his feet, but his argument fell on deaf ears.

Jesse shoved him aside and set off running after his phone. "I forgive you!" he hollered. "Come back!"

Shaking his head, Sam hurried into the garden, around the side of the house, then into Arty's shed. He wasn't really sure what all the stuff on Arty's list actually was, so he decided to grab one of everything and cram it all in his bag.

There was a set of blueprints for CHARLES spread out on the table, so he folded that up and shoved it into his bag, too.

Job done, he yanked open the shed door, darted out into the garden . . .

. . . and right into the path of a mean-looking lawn mower with murder on its mind.

Guide to Evil Sentient Technology

When the machines eventually take over—and they will, people, they will—some of them will obviously be of more concern than others. But how to tell which is which? Cut out this guide and keep it with you at all times so you can be better prepared.

Worrying Appliances

• Power tools of any kind

• Microwaves with the door open

• Cotton-candy machines

• Anything with lasers mounted on it

• Walk-in freezers with doors that open only from the outside

Less Worrying Appliances

- Shoe polisher

- Battery-operated child's fan

- Radios

- Bread makers

- Anything entirely encased in soft, squishy rubber

- Light-up sneakers (unless you're wearing them)

- Videocassette recorders from the 1980s

- Videocassette recorders from any other decade

- Motorized elbow ticklers (not a problem, because they don't exist)

CHAPTER EIGHT

Wow! I don't know about you, but I'm on the edge of my seat after that last chapter ending. I mean—Sam is face-to-face with a killer lawn mower! Well, not face-to-face obviously—lawn mowers don't have faces, but you know what I mean.

I can't wait to find out what happens to Sam next!

But, alas, I'm going to have to, and so are you, because we're whizzing back over to see what Emmie and Arty are up to instead. Hang in there, Sam—we'll be back soon!

Mostly what Emmie and Arty were up to was narrowly avoiding being blown to bits. Both

CHARLES and the soldiers were still shooting the place up with their lasers, locked in an epic battle that wouldn't have looked out of place in a Hollywood blockbuster, if I do say so myself.

Arty sort of wanted to hang around and see what happened, but as he's actually quite sensible by nature, he decided it was best to run away, instead. He followed Emmie as she went tearing up the steps of the Town Hall and barged in through the front door.

Sam had told his friends about the control room, so Emmie and Arty quickly made their way there. The control-room door was made of reinforced metal, with a little bulletproof window mounted in the middle. An eyeball scanner was built into the wall beside it so only authorized personnel could get inside. It would've been completely impossible to break into, were it not for one tiny detail.

"Someone's left the door open," Emmie said, stepping inside.

The control room was empty. Well, not *empty*. It had all the computers and desks and stuff. A rug and whatnot. In terms of objects and furniture, it was actually reasonably full. What it was distinctly lacking, though, was people.

"Where is everyone?" Arty gasped.

Emmie stepped farther into the room, casting her gaze across the banks of screens. The battle between CHARLES and the soldiers was raging, and for the first time, Emmie noticed that Earl Brute himself wasn't down there.

She had just begun to wonder where he might be, when Arty grabbed her by the arm. "Shh!" he hissed, despite the fact Emmie wasn't making a sound. "Listen!"

Emmie listened. All she could hear was the whirring of lots of computer fans and a faint hum from the lights overhead. But then she heard another noise, too: a muffled grunt, like someone had sealed a baboon in a bag and it wasn't pleased. It seemed to come from a door at the other end of the control room.

Slowly, Emmie and Arty approached the door.

"Mr. Saunders!" Arty cried as he and Emmie stepped through the door and into a very large closet.

Sure enough, Sam's dad was there, lying on the floor, his hands and feet tied together, and a piece of shiny silver tape across his mouth. What's more, he wasn't alone. The rest of the control room staff had all been tied up in similar ways, although one only had brown tape covering his mouth, and you could tell he was secretly quite jealous of the others.

"Lmm ouuu!" mumbled Mr. Saunders.

"What?" said Emmie.

"Lmm ouuu!"

Emmie and Arty exchanged a glance. Arty shrugged.

"We're not getting it," said Emmie. "Say it more slowly."

"Lmm."

"Right."

"Oouu!"

"Lmm oouu?" said Emmie.

Mr. Saunders nodded frantically.

Emmie turned to Arty again. "Any idea what 'lmm oouu' means?"

Arty shook his head. "Nope," he said. "We could always take the tape off."

"Good idea," said Emmie. She crossed the closet, then bent down and ripped off Mr. Saunders's tape in one quick yank. It was times like this, Mr. Saunders realized, he was glad he didn't have a mustache.

"Now," said Emmie, "what were you saying?"

"I was saying," began Mr. Saunders, "look out!"

Right then, there was the roar of something electrical springing to life. Arty and Emmie whipped around to see the office's paper shredder thundering across the floor, its metal teeth chewing hungrily.

The control-room staff wailed and wriggled,

desperately trying to get away from the approaching appliance.

The shredder dashed across the room like a hungry lion with metal teeth. It zigged and zagged across the floor, as if it couldn't quite decide who its first victim should be.

To Arty's dismay, it decided it should be him.

"G-get away!" he cried, trying to climb up a perfectly smooth wall to escape the shredder's deadly shreddy bit. "I'm too big; I'll get stuck in your teeth!"

"You heard him, shred-head!" Emmie snarled, hurling herself onto the machine and punching it repeatedly in its ribs. Or where its ribs would have been, if office paper shredders had any. (Which they don't, by the way—I've checked the manual.)

The shredder thrashed and bucked like an angry

bull, flipping and tossing Emmie around. She clung on tightly, hammering her fists against the machine in the hope of smashing something vital.

But then the shredder stopped suddenly, raising its bottom end into the air. Emmie was thrown into a clumsy somersault. She landed on her back on the carpet and craned her neck in time to see the shredder's metal teeth closing in fast.

Emmie covered her head with her hands. She shut her eyes.

Then she opened them again when the roaring of the shredder spluttered and died. Arty stood over by the wall, an electrical cord in his hand.

"I unplugged it," he said.

"Genius move, Arty!" cried Mr. Saunders.

Arty blinked. "Well, not really. It was pretty obvious, actually." He bent down to also open up the shredder's back and ripped out any electronic machinery—he didn't want to take any chances.

"What I want to know," said Mr. Saunders, as Arty untied him, "is how it came to life in the first place."

"It was CHARLES," Arty explained.

"Aha!" said Mr. Saunders, nodding sagely. "Who's CHARLES, then?"

"He's my robot."

"He's gone evil," Emmie explained. "He wants to clean us all out of existence, and he's taken control of all other electronics so that they'll help him."

"Well," Mr. Saunders huffed, standing up and rubbing the rope-marks on his wrists, "I'm sure Earl Brute has it all under control!"

"Erm, no. He's also evil," Emmie added. "He wants to take over the town and rule it with an iron fist. Sorry, I almost forgot that part."

"Right," said Mr. Saunders, trying very hard to smile, but not making a very good job of it. "Busy day ahead, then, what with one thing and another."

"Who tied you up, by the way?" Emmie asked.

"We don't know exactly," he said, setting to

work unraveling a colleague's knot. "They jumped us from behind."

"Minions!" Emmie guessed. Obviously Brute's soldiers had been hard at work.

When everyone else was untied, they headed back through to the control room. "We could use the lasers," Emmie said. "Blast CHARLES to bits."

"No!" Arty yelped. "We agreed. The plan is to keep him in one piece. He's my lovely electronic pal."

Emmie gestured to one of the monitors, where CHARLES was unleashing another volley of laser fire on Brute's minions. "Not anymore he isn't."

Suddenly, a flash of movement on another screen caught her eye. "Hey, look, there's Sam!" she said. They all gathered around the monitor to watch Sam racing across a lawn at blisteringly high speed.

"He's in a rush, isn't he?" said Arty. Then a quick glance at another screen revealed why. Charging up behind him was an out-of-control lawn mower.

"It's gaining on him!" cried Mr. Saunders. He began running in circles, because running in circles was his default way of dealing with emergency situations. "What will we do?"

Emmie slid onto a seat in front of a console. She took hold of a joystick. "We'll do this," she said, then gritted her teeth, shut one eye, and pressed the button.

CHAPTER NINE

Sam ran, using all his world-famous speed, but unfortunately it wasn't enough. He could hear the mower chewing up the ground behind him, getting steadily closer with every moment. He was still holding his baseball bat, but the lawn mower was built like a tank, and no amount of *thwacking* was going to put a dent in it.

Sam's life flashed before his eyes. The first few years weren't much to write home about, but the final few months were pretty flippin' exciting. If he had to go, he supposed being chewed to bits by an artificially intelligent lawn mower under the control of a massive robot made about as much sense as anything else.

But he wasn't going to just lie down and let it gobble him up. Sam ducked his head and kicked his legs for extra speed. He glanced back over his shoulder, sure he'd see the lawn mower falling behind. Instead, he saw it leaping into the air (surprisingly gracefully, he couldn't help but notice) and hurtling toward him.

Then, with a *bzzzt* and a *boom*, the lawn mower exploded. Sam stopped running and blinked in surprise. He glanced up and noticed one of the town's laser blasters. It looked like he had a guardian angel—a guardian angel with high-velocity laser-based weaponry, which really is the best kind of guardian angel.

From there, getting to the Town Hall was pretty easy. Oh sure, it looked like CHARLES had become even *more* powerful. In five minutes, he had eliminated our heroes' best defense strategy (you know, the one Arty so masterfully demonstrated in the last chapter)—the machines were now running rampant *without* being plugged in! Sam had to dodge the odd killer kitchen appliance and jump over a particularly unhappy-looking hair dryer, but none of it proved to be too much of a problem.

He reached the bottom steps just as Arty and Emmie opened the Town Hall's front door.

"About time!" Emmie cried.

"I got a little held up." Sam laughed.

But before he could bound up the steps, something buzzed at Sam's head. He ducked, but not before a few stray strands of hair were snipped off by whatever had dive-bombed him. Sam watched his lovely locks float off on the breeze, then turned

in time for a little helicopter drone to swoop at him once again.

"Wargh!" he cried, ducking just as its spinning blades tried to hack his face to bits.

Sam straightened up into a swing, bringing his baseball bat swooping upward. It hit the drone with an almighty *ker-ack*, sending the whirring machine spinning up into the sky and then hurtling down to the ground again. It exploded on the steps right in front of Arty, making him jump in fright, and—if he was honest—wet himself just a tiny bit.

"Quick, get in," Emmie urged, scanning the skies.

Sam scampered up the last few steps and stumbled through the door. Arty and Emmie hurriedly pushed it closed, and they all slumped down against the wood.

"There's a lot of weird stuff going on out there," Sam said, through big shaky breaths.

"Yeah, we noticed," said Emmie.

"We think CHARLES *may* have a hand in it," said Arty.

Emmie shot him a withering look.

"Okay, it's definitely CHARLES," Arty admitted. "He's controlling all the other appliances via Bluetooth, which is very clever, if I do say so myself."

"Yes, well done, Arty," said Emmie, patting him on the back more violently than he'd have liked. "Your robot has now got a whole army of electronic equipment trying to clean us out of existence. You must be very proud!"

Arty *was* quite proud, actually. I mean, yes, CHARLES had turned into a relentless cleaning machine of destruction with no concept of mercy, but he was *definitely* more impressive than a rotating hat with mirrors on it.

Sam tipped his backpack up, spilling circuit boards, microchips, tools, and other fancy stuff onto the floor. "I brought everything I could find," he said, passing Arty the rolled-up blueprints.

"The first part of making CHARLES nice

again is easy," said Arty. His lips kept moving
and he said a load of science things that went
completely over Sam's and Emmie's heads. They
nodded along like they understood it but secretly
had no idea what he was talking about. He may as
well have just been saying, "Science stuff, science

stuff, science stuff," over and over again, as far as they were concerned.

By the time they'd finished nodding blankly at him, Arty held up a little gizmo he'd made from circuit boards, microchips, and one of those knobbly bits with the wires at either end.

"Ta-daa!" he said, beaming proudly. "What do you think?"

"What *is* that?" Emmie asked.

"It's a *down*grader upgrade," said Arty. "We just upload this into CHARLES; it'll reconfigure his scrambled programming and return him back to his harmless old self."

"Sounds easy," said Emmie.

"It is!" Arty said. "Sort of," he added. "A bit." He chewed his lip. "Not really."

"How come?" asked Sam.

Arty took a deep breath. "Because to make it work, we have to plug this directly into CHARLES's hardware, which involves getting on his back, unscrewing four screws, removing a security plate, swapping out the old chip, and plugging this one in in its place."

"Oh," said Sam, who had been dead optimistic a minute ago but was suddenly feeling quite a bit less so. "Still, it sounds doable."

"It is," said Arty. "It absolutely is. Except . . ."

Emmie groaned. "What now?"

"Except, from the moment we get those screws off, we have only thirty seconds to make the swap."

"Or it won't work?" said Sam.

Arty smiled shakily. "Or CHARLES will activate his self-destruct sequence, and everything inside Sitting Duck will be blown to bits!"

CHAPTER TEN

Sam and Emmie were sitting with their backs against the door, quietly contemplating the significance of what Arty had said at the end of that last chapter, when suddenly the door flew open, sending all three children rolling across the floor.

They jumped to their feet (well, Arty sort of clambered slowly) to see Earl Brute in the doorway. The head of security's face was fixed in an angry grimace, but then, that was pretty much his default look ever since that fateful day several years previously, when the wind had changed just as Brute had made that very face. He'd been stuck with it ever since.

As it happened, though, even if his face hadn't

been stuck in that expression, he'd still be doing that same expression right now anyway, because Earl Brute was furious.

"There's a great big robot tearing up the town!" he barked. "It's about time I take charge in the interests of public safety."

"In the interests of public *un*safety, you mean," said Mr. Saunders, racing down the stairs. It was probably one of the worst comebacks in the history of the world, just behind "I know you are, but what am I?"

Mr. Saunders squared his shoulders and pointed an accusing finger at the head of security. "Earl Brute, step back, you are relieved of your duty!" he said.

Sam raised his eyebrows, surprised to see his usually mild-mannered dad standing up to the much bigger Brute.

"No," said Brute.

Mr. Saunders blinked. "What?"

"No," repeated Brute, stepping in close and looming over poor Mr. Saunders. His mustache twitched. "This town is now under our control."

Mr. Saunders swallowed. "Um . . . what? You mean you and me?"

"No. I mean me and them," said Brute, jabbing a thumb toward the door just as four of his minions came strutting in like they owned the place. They all had mean-looking laser blasters to go with their mean-looking faces, and all Mr. Saunders's bravery seemed to evaporate the moment he set eyes on them.

"Right. Gotcha!" he said, sweating heavily. "Good luck with it all, in that case!"

"I don't need luck," Brute growled. "My team and I are going to blast that hunk of junk into tiny bits and keep this town safe."

Arty raised a hand. "No, you don't have to—"

"Then blast those tiny bits into even tinier bits."

"Yes, but—"

"Then take those even tinier bits, and mash them up into a fine dust."

Arty opened his mouth to speak, realized it was pointless, and closed it again. Brute had made up his mind. He was going to destroy CHARLES, and there was nothing Arty could do to convince him otherwise.

Suddenly, the windows of the Town Hall dimmed, as if the morning sun had dropped behind a curtain of black cloud.

"That's strange," Sam muttered. "There wasn't a cloud in the sky a minute ago."

The floor trembled beneath their feet. Arty glanced down, then up at the darkened window. "I d-don't think that's a cloud," he whispered.

"ATTENTION, HUMAN OCCUPANTS OF THE TOWN HALL," boomed a voice, so loud it made the windows rattle and the lamp shades shake. "COME OUT NOW, OR I WILL DESTROY THE BUILDING."

"I bet that's the robot," said Brute, who had a real knack of stating the obvious. Rolling up his sleeves, he marched toward the door. "Come watch me blast this thing into next week!"

Surrounded by the armed men, Sam and the others headed outside. Brute stood on the steps, his mouth open, his eyes wide, and his head tilted back as he looked up at the gigantic clutter of metal that towered above him.

CHARLES's head and face were the same as ever, but his body had grown to almost twice its height and width, and he had armored himself with fancy metal.

Arty dabbed at his eyes and sniffed. "They grow up so fast."

"What should we do, sir?" asked one of the armed men. Earl Brute didn't respond, though. He just stood there, his eyes bulging, his mouth

still hanging open, almost like he'd never seen a freaking-enormous killer robot before.

Arty saw his chance. He stepped in front of Brute and flashed CHARLES a warm smile. "Hey, pal!" he said. "It's me—Arty!"

The expression lit up on CHARLES's face didn't flicker.

"What's the matter? Don't you recognize me?" Arty said. "Remember all those good times we had? Going to the science fair . . . and,

you know, we probably did some other stuff, too."

"Recognize," chimed CHARLES.

"Yes!" Arty cheered.

"Recognize contamination," CHARLES continued. "Contamination must be destroyed."

"No!" Arty wailed.

Sam and Emmie caught Arty by the arms and guided him back a few paces. Behind CHARLES, dozens of photocopiers, washing machines, coffee machines, and bread makers all hopped, wobbled, teetered, and bounced up the steps, all controlled by his electrical wizardry. In moments, the entrance to the Town Hall was completely surrounded.

"Sir?" said one of the soldiers, his finger tightening on the trigger of his laser blaster. "What should we do?"

"Um . . ." said Earl Brute, which wasn't particularly helpful for anyone. "Um . . . Um . . ."

"Blast it?" asked the minion.

Brute nodded frantically. "Y-yes. Blast it."

The soldiers pointed their blasters at CHARLES. They squeezed the triggers. Laser fire erupted from the barrels, then bounced harmlessly off him.

"Didn't work, sir," said the soldier. "Any other ideas?"

Brute shook his head. "N-not really," he admitted.

Just then, Mr. Saunders stepped forward, taking charge. "Concentrate your fire on that area," he said, pointing to what looked like a weak spot near CHARLES's neck. "Don't stop shooting until—"

Suddenly four long power cords wrapped around the soldiers' legs, yanking them off the ground and flicking them through the air. They screamed as they flailed across the sky, and then went *zzzap* when they hit the electrified dome, exploding in a shower of blue sparks.

Mr. Saunders cleared his throat. He smiled vaguely at CHARLES. "Just kidding," he squeaked, then darted back into the Town Hall, raced through to his office, and took cover beneath his desk.

Back outside, Sam, Arty, and Emmie were desperately searching for a way to escape. Brute, on the other hand, was still just staring blankly up at the enormous robot. His hard-man act had collapsed, and now he looked on the brink of bursting into tears. Even his mustache had stopped bristling and was now sagging like an old dog on a hot day.

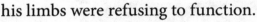

"Well, go on, then, Brute!" Sam urged. "Do something."

"C-can't," Brute whispered. It looked like he was completely immobilized by fear and his limbs were refusing to function.

Actually, that turned out not to be true. When CHARLES reshaped his arms into an enormous dustpan and brush and made a move to sweep Brute up, the head of security erupted into a chorus of high-pitched screams, vaulted over an approaching fridge-freezer, and then raced into the distance, his arms flailing madly in the air.

"Wow," muttered Arty as he, Sam, and Emmie watched Brute go. "They don't make overprotective tyrants like they used to, do they?"

Charles Character Profile
(Upgraded Version)

- Massive.

- Like, *really* massive.

- Seriously, look at him. He's huge.

- Laser eyes that could burn your face off.

- Insanely advanced artificial intelligent chip, getting smarter by the second.

- Upgraded LED face, able to show up to *four* emotions at once.

- Shape-shifting metal components let him take any form, as long as it's a massive robot.

- Hammer attachment, for hammering.

- Detachable right leg to use as a golf club, perfect for unwinding after a hard day's laser blasting.

CHAPTER ELEVEN

Earl Brute was gone. His minions? Also gone. Sam, Arty, and Emmie? Right there, and ready to fight for Sitting Duck like the awesome heroes they are.

A fax machine—which didn't realize quite how awesome the friends were—decided to try roughing them up. It lunged at them, swinging its paper tray (which was quite dusty, because it hadn't been used since the olden days).

Quick as a flash, Sam leaped back, spun around with his bat, and slammed it into the side of the machine, which exploded into a shower of flimsy plastic and—strangely—jelly beans.

Sam hoped that display of butt-kickery would

put the other machines off, but all around the semicircle of out-of-control tech, motors revved, components whirred, and bleepy things went *bleep*.

"It's no use," said Emmie. "There are too many of them, and we've only got one bat."

Sam punched his fist into his palm. "If only there was a way of destroying them more easily."

Arty raised a finger. "Um . . ."

"You're right," said Emmie. "Some means of blasting them to bits while we stayed relatively safe in, like, a room or somewhere."

"Um . . ."

"In like some sort of control room," said Sam. "Where we could remotely operate some sort of, I don't know, let's just for the sake of argument say laser-based weaponry."

"Um . . ."

Emmie rounded on Arty. "Why do you keep saying 'Um'?"

Arty's eyes flicked to an upstairs window of the Town Hall. Sam and Emmie both followed his gaze, and then slapped themselves on the forehead at exactly the same time.

"Arty, you're a genius!" Sam cried as they turned back toward the door.

"Well, yes," Arty agreed. "But I don't think I really needed to be the one to figure that out."

Slamming and locking the door behind them, Sam, Arty, and Emmie tore up the stairs and barged into the control room. The console operators had all barricaded themselves into the little room at the back, leaving the controls free for Sam, Emmie, and Arty.

"It's really easy," said Emmie, who—because she'd fired one laser blaster that one time, suddenly considered herself an expert on the subject. Which was fair enough, actually, because she had managed to hit a moving target on her first try, which was more than any of the actual operators had ever done, so good on her, I say. "You just aim with the joystick, press the button, and BOOM!"

They all plonked themselves onto different seats and turned their lasers to point at the electronic army outside. "Don't destroy CHARLES," Arty urged. "I can still fix him."

"Go for his friends, then," said Sam, positioning his crosshairs over a particularly aggressive-looking microwave. He pushed the button, and there was a powerful blast of absolutely nothing whatsoever.

Sam pressed again. "Huh? Nothing's happening," he said.

"Same here," said Emmie, and then she yelped as the joystick moved suddenly on its own. On-screen, she saw her laser blaster open fire on Sam's, which promptly exploded with a *bang*.

"You shot my blaster!" Sam protested.

"It wasn't me," said Emmie. "It did it itself."

"No, it didn't," said Arty. He was wrestling with the controls of his own blaster, but he wasn't strong enough to stop it swiveling and blowing Emmie's to bits. "It's CHARLES. He's taken control of the zombie-defense lasers."

"Oh, well, that's just great!" Sam groaned. "How are we supposed to destroy his army now?"

"We have to think of something low-tech," said Arty.

"Pudding!" suggested Emmie.

"Not that low tech," said Arty.

"I've still got my baseball bat," said Sam. For the first time ever, he was pleased his mom and dad had refused to pay for the extra-deluxe bat he'd pestered them for, with built-in Wi-Fi and Bluetooth dongles. That would've been disastrous, given the current predicament.

"That won't get us very far," said Emmie. "Some of that stuff looks pretty unsmashable."

Arty stood up and began to pace the room, deep in thought. "It doesn't have to be a weapon. We just need a way to distract CHARLES long enough for me to—"

If Arty finished the sentence, no one heard it. They were too busy screaming in panic as the control room window and a big piece of the wall exploded. Sam, Arty, and Emmie stumbled back just as an enormous robotic hand reached through the hole.

"Back off, CHARLES!" Sam yelped, thwacking one of the metal fingers with his bat. CHARLES didn't seem too upset about it, though, and kept reaching for them anyway.

The three friends tripped and staggered out

of the room, then tumbled clumsily down the stairs. They lay in a heap at the bottom, panting and wheezing, their hearts jackhammering like jackhammers in their chests.

"I've got it!" cried Arty.

"If by 'it' you mean 'mild concussion,' I think I've got it, too," muttered Emmie, rubbing the back of her head.

"No," Arty cried. "I mean I know how we can stop CHARLES."

"How?" asked Sam.

Arty held up the little gizmo he'd made. "With *this*!"

Emmie and Sam exchanged a worried glance. "Yeah, he's definitely hit his head," said Sam.

"You told us that earlier," Emmie pointed out.

Arty blinked. "Did I?" His shoulders sagged. "Oh. Right. Why didn't we use it then?"

"Because we can't get close enough to get on CHARLES's back," Emmie said. "Remember?"

"Not really," said Arty, gingerly rubbing a lump on the back of his head. "Why didn't we just distract him with something?"

"Distract who?" asked Sam.

"CHARLES," said Arty.

Sam hesitated. "I don't know. Why *didn't* we just distract him with something?"

"Pudding!" cried Emmie, who kept bringing the subject up only because she hadn't eaten all morning, and now quite fancied the idea of some lovely chocolate pudding.

"Wait! What about the science fair?" said Sam.

Arty sighed. "Yes, I know, I didn't win. No need to rub it in."

"No, I mean . . . apart from Arty, most of the stuff there was terrible, right?" said Sam. "Like Emmie's alarm thingy."

"Hey!" said Emmie. "But you're right; it was terrible, yeah."

"And as for that mirror hat!" snorted Arty. "I mean, that was just ludicrous. It's a hat with mirrors on it. Where's the science in that?"

"Yes, yes, shut up," said Emmie. "You should have won. We get it."

"But," Sam began, "would the alarm and mirror hat be enough to distract him?"

"No. Definitely not," said Arty.

Sam and Emmie both groaned.

"Wait, that came out wrong. I meant almost certainly yes," said Arty, who always got those two mixed up. "Those should confuse his sensors, but it wouldn't give us long."

"It's the big game today," said Sam. He looked at his watch. "It's starting soon."

"Yes, well, I think you'll probably have to miss it," said Arty, a little bit annoyed that his friend had changed the subject.

"No, I mean everyone will be gathering. That's where Phoebe will be," said Sam.

"She's bound to have her stupid hat with her," said Emmie. "She'll be showing that thing off for months."

Sam raced to the door, his baseball bat raised. "Then let's go," he said. "Ready?"

The others nodded. "Ready," they said.

Together they bounded outside to punch, kick,

and baseball-bat their way through the crowd of machinery.

At the field, the bleachers were already filling up with townsfolk, none of whom seemed to be all that bothered that their appliances had both come to life and turned evil at the same time. The people of Sitting Duck had put up with a lot worse over the past few months, so I suppose you can't really blame them for just wanting to enjoy a nice day out at the ball game now, can you?

Sam, Arty, and Emmie scanned the area. They spotted lots of familiar faces. There was Old Mrs. Missus, Werewolf Alan, and the Kevin twins from chapter four. Over there was Mr. Nerdgoober from chapter one. It was a bit like a mini-reunion of all the minor characters from the story so far, and a whole host of new friendly faces as well—including the visiting team and their fans. Something glinted as it reflected the sunlight a few rows from the back of the stands.

"There!" cried Emmie, stabbing a finger toward Phoebe. She was perched on a bench, her stupid hat stuck on her stupid head, mirrors whirling around and around like a tiny fairground ride. "I found her."

"Unfortunately," said Arty, his voice shaking, "someone else has found *us*."

Sam and Emmie both turned. Their hearts leaped into their mouths. Not literally, though, because that's gross.

They got scared is what I'm trying to say.

There, striding, hopping, rolling, and shuffling toward them, was CHARLES and his army of decidedly unlovely electronic pals.

CHAPTER TWELVE

I'm pretty sure I've already mentioned this, but the residents of Sitting Duck had put up with a lot of nonsense over the last few months. You'd think they'd be pretty used to insane life-or-death situations by now, wouldn't you?

But no.

They could handle a few rogue appliances, but when CHARLES appeared it all turned to chaos. The whole crowd started screaming and wailing and running around in panic. A few people fainted in terror. Some were so scared they puked on themselves, but let's not dwell too much on that, because it's not nice to look at and a bit smelly.

Sam, Arty, and Emmie were separated by

the throngs of thrashing scaredy-cats. Sam clambered up the side of the bleachers, trying to get to Phoebe. As luck would have it, she was so transfixed by her own reflection, she'd completely failed to notice that anything was happening at all.

Sam hurried toward her, fighting his way against the tide of fleeing bodies. Behind him, CHARLES reached an enormous hand down and snatched up Hot-Dog Dan the Hot-Dog Man's hot-dog stand. It was shaped like an enormous hot-dog bun, and Dan was squashed into the middle like a sausage.

"Mmm. This look delicious *and* nutritious," CHARLES said, in a voice that rolled like thunder across the sky. Hot-Dog Dan was about to live up to his name.

CHARLES was just opening his metallic

mouth, ready to chomp down on the human-y
hot dog, when a high-pitched screech split the air.
His LED eyes blinked in surprise, and he turned
slowly, searching for the source of the sound.

Emmie stood before him, holding up the alien-
detecting alarm she'd built. It was screeching
even though there were no aliens present,

but that's because it wasn't really an alien-detecting alarm at all. Emmie had just said that to get extra credit at the science fair. The alarm was actually activated by a big red button with ACTIVATE ALARM written on it.

CHARLES reached for the screeching siren, letting Hot-Dog Dan the Hot-Dog Man tumble back to the ground. Hot-Dog Dan bounced off the floor, squashing a huge tub of ketchup that sent bright red goop splashing across the ground.

Emmie ducked and darted out of CHARLES's reach, forcing him to bend lower. Seizing his opportunity, Arty hurled himself onto the back of his robot's leg. Despite not being the most athletic person in the world (or even in the top six billion), Arty knew the fate of everyone in Sitting Duck rested on his shoulders.

Clenching his downgrader gizmo between his teeth, Arty reached up and slowly began to climb.

"Yoink!" cried Sam, snaffling the hat off Phoebe's head. She blinked in surprise and tried to grab it back. Only then did she spot the enormous robot and realize that the rest of the crowd had fled in panic.

Phoebe sighed. "OMG, not another end-of-the-world thing?"

"'Fraid so," said Sam. "We need your hat."

"Like, whatever," Phoebe said. "Just try not to turn me into a zombie this time, mmmkay?"

"I'll do my best," said Sam.

He gave her a nod and then turned back toward CHARLES. He was bending over, trying to grab the fast-moving Emmie and her earsplitting alarm. The top of the robot's head was more or less level with the top of the bleachers.

Sam rocked on his heels and took a few deep breaths. (Four, if you were wondering how many.) He would get only one chance at this. If he failed, then the town was done for.

He couldn't hesitate, couldn't hold back. He just had to go for it. There was no other choice. He just had to go.

He had to get it done.

No more hanging around.

There was a job to do, and he was going to do it.

This was it.

The moment of truth.

No time to wa—

"Oh, get on with it!" Phoebe cried.

Sam launched himself along the bleachers,

bounding onto the seats and racing as fast as his legs would carry him. CHARLES's head was a dozen yards away now. Eight. Four. One!

Sam leaped through the air.

CHARLES, detecting the human child sailing toward him, looked up. His eyes blazed red as his lasers locked on Sam.

"Keep your hat on, CHARLES!" Sam quipped (it sounded funnier when he said it) as he plonked the mirror hat on the robot's metal skull. It didn't fit quite right, but Sam managed to set it at a stylish, jaunty angle.

The mirrors jiggled around on their little arms, and CHARLES was immediately transfixed. "Targets identified," he began, but then he fell silent and knelt down, admiring his own robotic face.

Sam bounced off CHARLES's shoulder and plunged toward the ground. Luckily, several hundred hot-dog buns and a pool of ketchup had spilled out all over it, which nicely cushioned his fall.

Emmie helped him to his feet, and they both stared up at Arty, who had now crawled halfway up CHARLES's back.

"It's all up to him now," Sam said.

Arty was trying not to let the pressure get to him. He'd never really seen himself as the brave hero type—that was Sam and Emmie's job—but right now there was no one else who could save the day.

Reaching into his pocket, he pulled out something that looked a bit like a screwdriver. It was a screwdriver, actually, which explains the similarity. His hands shook as he undid the four screws holding the access panel in place.

"Here goes," he muttered, then pried the panel off. Immediately, a little speaker built into CHARLES's back crackled into life.

"Self-destruct countdown initiated," said a high-pitched voice. "Ten seconds until detonation."

"I knew that was a bad idea," Arty said, cursing himself for filling CHARLES's legs with enough explosives to level half the town.

Arty's fingers trembled as he yanked out the old wiring.

"Five," chimed the voice. "Four. Three."

Finally, he gained access to CHARLES's chip.

"Two."

Arty yanked out the upgrade chip.

"One."

With a frantic yelp, he shoved his gadgety-gizmo doohickey into the slot.

And CHARLES exploded.

Only he didn't. Not really. Not in a self-destruct *kaboom* kind of way. Instead, the additional pieces he'd attached to himself fell away at once. They rained like massive metal raindrops, squashing the electrical appliances below.

Arty fell, but luckily no one had tidied away all those hot dog buns yet, so they cushioned his fall, too.

(Ah, hot dogs. Is there nothing they can't do?)

With a soft *bump*, CHARLES landed on the ground between Arty and his friends. His LED smile was warm and welcoming, his eyes were very definitely *not* shooting lasers all over the place, and he was back to his normal size.

"Hello, friends," said CHARLES as Sam, Arty, and Emmie looked at him with relief. "This place looks like it could use some tidying up!"

CHAPTER THIRTEEN

The next day, things were already getting back to normal. Emmie was out early walking Attila the cat in Hetchley's Park, and Sam and Arty had decided to join her. Arty had brought CHARLES, too, because he was back to being his friendly old self now and wasn't showing any signs of wanting to clean everyone out of existence.

Sam was disappointed that he didn't get to play in the ball game, but on the other hand he was pretty pleased that they'd successfully saved Sitting Duck from danger yet again. His dad had let Sam keep the game ball, once he'd finally climbed out from under his desk. He'd said it was the least the town's residents could do to show their thanks.

The three friends were strolling through the park, enjoying the peace and quiet. Most of the machines in town had gone back to their normal selves, and stillness had fallen over the town like a blanket. But a blanket made of silence, if you can imagine such a thing.

Except . . .

Everything wasn't *quite* silent. There was a muffled sobbing coming from somewhere in the park. Sam looked around, searching for the source of it, before finally pinpointing the culprit.

Earl Brute was hidden high in the leaves of a tree, clinging on to a branch like his life depended on it.

"Hey there," Sam called.

"G-get that th-thing away!" Brute wailed, glaring in terror at CHARLES.

"I'm your electronic pal," CHARLES chimed, but from the way Brute sobbed hysterically, it was clear he wasn't convinced.

"Oh, while you're up there," Sam began, "we need the remote control for the doors. Sitting Duck doesn't need to be under an electrified dome anymore, really."

"Wh-what?" Brute stammered. "No! It's dangerous out there."

"It's more dangerous in here," said Emmie, unclipping Attila's leash. The cat hissed at her, then immediately shot up the tree.

Brute screamed as he released his grip and plunged to the ground. Attila scampered back down the tree after him, and clamped himself to

Brute's face, tail wrapped around his throat like the angriest and tightest scarf in the world.

"Mmmf mmmf ummpf!" Brute mumbled, searching frantically in his pockets. He tossed the remote control onto the grass, then got up and ran off, Attila still holding tightly to his head.

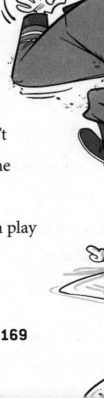

"At least now we can open the doors," said Sam.

"At least now we don't have to keep walking the cat," said Emmie.

"At least now we can play some ball," said Arty.

Sam looked at his friend and frowned. "What?"

"I feel bad for making you miss the game yesterday," Arty said.

Emmie snorted. "Why, because you built a living robot that tried to destroy us all?"

"Yes, because of that," said Arty, blushing slightly. "So, I thought I'd make some modifications to CHARLES."

Emmie and Sam both groaned. "What is it this time?" Emmie asked. "Human-seeking missiles? Child-chomping jaws?"

A panel on CHARLES's chest unfolded and a baseball bat attachment swung out. Arty grinned. "Not quite," he said.

"Cool!" laughed Sam. "Looks like I'm going to get a game after all."

"We shouldn't be playing. We should be figuring out a way to destroy the dome," Emmie said.

"Then watch this."

Sam grabbed the spare baseball from his backpack and took a few steps back. With all the strength he could muster, he tossed the ball to CHARLES. The robot swung and connected with a *ker-ack* that shook all the leaves off the nearest trees.

Sam, Arty, and Emmie watched the ball rocket through the air, high above the rooftops of Sitting Duck. With a sonic boom, the ball broke the sound barrier, and the reinforced glass dome, too.

"I don't think we need to worry about that," said Sam, grinning happily. "I'd say demolition has already begun!"

Read them all!

Disaster strikes the town of Sitting Duck again . . . and again . . . and again. . . .

DISASTER DIARIES

ALIENS!

**Read on for a sneaky look at the disaster-
defeating wisdom you don't want to miss
out on in this book. . . .**

Sam, Arty, and Emmie have barely gotten
over a recent zombie infestation when their
sleepy little town finds itself the victim of
an alien invasion!

But the aliens are very small and kind of,
well, cute—how dangerous can they be?

SPOILER ALERT: They're VERY dangerous.
And when they disintegrate the mayor with
their ray guns, it'll be up to Sam, Arty, and
Emmie to save the day. Again.

Defend Yourself from an Alien Sneak Attack

So aliens have invaded your planet? Bummer. Don't worry, I've put together this list of techniques you might want to put into use should one of those pesky invaders try to kill you in unpleasant ways. Be aware that some of these techniques will only be effective against specific alien races. While it is possible, for example, to tickle a member of the Fluffpuffle race into submission, this strategy will be somewhat less effective against the captain of a Venusian Death Fleet.

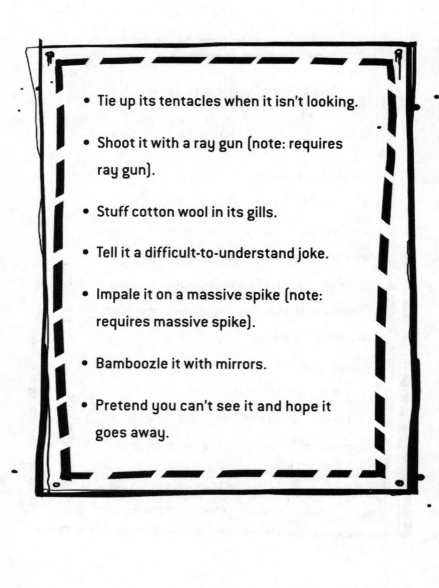

- Tie up its tentacles when it isn't looking.

- Shoot it with a ray gun (note: requires ray gun).

- Stuff cotton wool in its gills.

- Tell it a difficult-to-understand joke.

- Impale it on a massive spike (note: requires massive spike).

- Bamboozle it with mirrors.

- Pretend you can't see it and hope it goes away.

DISASTER DIARIES

BRAINWASHED!

Read on for a sneaky look at the disaster-defeating wisdom you don't want to miss out on in another book. . . .

Ravenous zombie hordes and swarms of power-hungry tiny aliens are just some of the disasters the town of Sitting Duck has faced.

But danger never sleeps and a new evil genius has arisen, and he's planning world domination with the aid of his homemade brainwashing device! Are Sam, Arty, and Emmie brave enough to save the day for the third time in a row?

If they aren't, everyone—including you, dear reader—will totally lose their minds!

HELP! My Friend Has Been Brainwashed!

So a friend or family member has been brainwashed and you're not sure what to do. Have no fear! Here are some possible suggestions for ways you might deal with them:

1. Lock them in a cupboard.

2. Lock them in a different cupboard.

3. Tie them to a tree.

4. Stuff their ears with cotton balls so they can't hear any commands.

5. Remove their eyes so they can't see any commands, either.

6. Actually, forget that last one. Get a blindfold. Much less messy.

HELP! I Want to Brainwash My Friend!

Oh, it's like that, is it? You want to try brainwashing your friend or family member to do your bidding? You naughty person, you. Well, some of these might help . . .

1. Wave your hands about in front of their face and say "Do as you are bid!" in a spooky voice.

2. Jab them repeatedly with your finger while going, "Are you brainwashed yet? Are you brainwashed yet? Are you brainwashed yet?" over and over again.

3. Invest billions of dollars in the development of a state-of-the-art brainwashing hypno-ray device. Or, alternatively . . .

4. Buy a pocket watch on a chain and swing it back and forth before their eyes.

5. Record yourself whispering "You shall obey my every command" and play it on a loop while they're sleeping.

Create a Disaster Survival Kit

What would you put in your own Disaster Survival Kit?

Maybe, like Arty, a Bristly Brain Basher
(aka toilet brush) is all you need to keep
enemies at bay?

Can you invent a more sophisticated form of weaponry
using a toilet roll or an empty cookie tin?

Or do you really just want some sweets and a clean T-shirt?

Pack your bag for the apocalypse and
keep it by the door in case of disaster!

About the Author

R. McGeddon is absolutely sure the world is almost certainly going to end very soon. A strange, reclusive fellow—so reclusive, in fact, that no one has ever seen him, not even his mom—he plots his stories using letters cut from old newspapers and types them up on an encrypted typewriter. It's also believed that he goes by other names, including A. Pocalypse and N. Dov Days, but since no one has ever met him in real life, it's hard to say for sure. One thing we know is when the apocalypse comes, he'll be ready!